Topsy Tim

and the new puppy

Jean and Gareth Adamson

PUFFIN BOOKS

PUFFIN BOOKS

Published by the Penguin Group
Penguin Books Ltd, 27 Wrights Lane, London W8 5TZ, England
Penguin Books USA Inc., 375 Hudson Street, New York, NY 10014, USA
Penguin Books Australia Ltd, Ringwood, Victoria, Australia
Penguin Books Canada Ltd, 10 Alcorn Avenue, Toronto, Ontario, Canada M4V 3B2
Penguin Books (NZ) Ltd, 182–190 Wairau Road, Auckland 10, New Zealand

Penguin Books Ltd, Registered Offices: Harmondsworth, Middlesex, England

First published by Blackie Children's Books 1994
Reissued in Puffin Books 1996
1 3 5 7 9 10 8 6 4 2

Copyright © Jean and Gareth Adamson, 1994
All rights reserved.

Made and printed in Great Britain by William Clowes Limited, Beccles and London

One day Topsy and Tim met their
schoolfriend, Louise Lewis. She was
with her dog, Poppy. Topsy patted
Poppy.
'Isn't she getting fat,' said Tim.
'That's because she has some puppies
inside her, waiting to be born,' said
Louise.

A few days later, Louise phoned Topsy and Tim. She sounded very excited. 'Poppy has had four puppies,' she told them. 'Would you like to come and see them?'

Mummy took Topsy and Tim to Louise's
house that afternoon.
'The puppies are in the kitchen,' said
Louise. 'I'll show them to you, but you
must be quiet.'

Poppy was lying on her side in a big box, well padded with newspaper. Four tiny puppies lay in a row, sucking milk from Poppy.

'Poppy's puppies don't look a bit like Poppy,' said Tim.

'Look, their eyes are shut,' said Topsy.
'They're drinking in their sleep.'
'They are awake,' said Louise's mum,
'but puppies don't open their eyes until
they are about ten days old.'

The next time Topsy and Tim went to
Louise's house, the puppies had opened
their eyes. They were growing plump,
but their legs were still weak and
wobbly. Topsy and Tim and Louise
played with the puppies for a while.

'We are going to keep one puppy,' said
Louise's mum, 'but we have to find
homes for the other three.'
'I wish we could have one,' said Topsy.

When the puppies were old enough they
were allowed to run about with Louise
and Topsy and Tim in the garden.
One puppy was so eager to run and play
he always seemed to be tumbling over.
Topsy and Tim called him Roly Poly.

'How much would you like a puppy of
our very own?' Topsy asked Tim.
Tim thought for a long time.
'I'd like one more than anything in the
whole world,' he said.

That night at bedtime Topsy and Tim asked Mummy and Dad if they could have one of Poppy's puppies.
'A puppy is fun,' said Mummy, 'but puppies soon grow up and a dog needs a lot of looking after.'

'If we had a puppy would you help look after it?' said Dad.
'Oh, we would,' promised Topsy and Tim.
'Do you know which one you would like?' asked Dad.
Topsy and Tim did know. 'We want Roly Poly' they said, both together.

Dad went downstairs. Topsy and Tim heard him talking on the telephone. He came back upstairs. 'I've just phoned Louise's mum,' he said. 'She's already found homes for two of the pups. There's only one left.' 'Which one?' asked Topsy and Tim. 'Roly Poly,' said Dad, 'and he's all yours.' Topsy and Tim slept with big smiles on their faces that night.

So, when he was old enough to leave his
mother, Roly Poly came to live with
Topsy and Tim. They loved looking
after him. He played a lot, slept a lot
and had lots of little meals. They had to
feed him four times a day and make
sure he had plenty of water to drink.

He was very naughty, too. He chased
Kitty and drank her milk. He barked at
Wiggles and he chewed up all Topsy
and Tim's shoes. Worst of all, he kept
making puddles on the floor.

After every meal Topsy and Tim took
him into the garden. When he did his
poos and puddles in the garden, they
said, 'Good boy, Roly Poly,' and patted
him. But he often made another puddle
when he came in.

Clever Kitty miaowed at the door when
she needed to go outside.
'I wish you would learn to ask to go out,
Roly,' said Topsy sadly, after Roly Poly
had made his third puddle on the floor.

At last Roly Poly understood. He went to the back door and barked. When Tim let him out, he made a big puddle in the garden. Topsy and Tim felt so proud, they phoned Louise to tell her the good news.

When he was twelve weeks old, Mummy took Roly Poly to the vet for his special injections against dog diseases. Louise went too, with her puppy, Daisy.
Roly Poly and Daisy were pleased to see each other.

'Soon Roly Poly and Daisy can go to
training classes,' said Louise's mum.
'What for?' asked Tim.
'So that they can learn to be good dogs
and do what we ask them,' said Louise's
mum.

The first training class was great fun.
Roly Poly and Daisy liked meeting all
the other dogs. The teacher showed
Topsy and Tim how to make Roly Poly
sit, stay and come when they called him.

'Sit!' said Topsy, but Roly Poly wouldn't.
'Stay!' said Tim, but Roly Poly didn't.
'Come!' said Topsy and Tim – and Roly
Poly did.
'He's doing very well,' said the teacher.

Dad came to take them home.
'Is Roly Poly trained now?' he asked.
'Er – not quite,' said Topsy and Tim.